"Who's the Diabetic Fish?"

All in a Day's Nursing:
A Tribute, With Songs

by
Ray Leonardsson

**Grosvenor House
Publishing Limited**

The right of Ray Leonardsson to be identified as the author of this
work has been asserted in accordance with Section 78
of the Copyright, Designs and Patents Act 1988

The book cover is copyright to Ray Leonardsson
Cover illustration is copyright to Peter Clayton

This book is published by
Grosvenor House Publishing Ltd
Link House
140 The Broadway, Tolworth, Surrey, KT6 7HT.
www.grosvenorhousepublishing.co.uk

Although inspired by real events,
this book is a work of fiction, and any resemblance
to people of events, past or present, is purely coincidental.

A CIP record for this book
is available from the British Library

ISBN 978-1-83975-709-9

Enjoy the read!

Ray

'Who's the Diabetic Fish?' is dedicated to all
the wonderful health professionals who work
within the NHS, and specifically to all the colleagues
who have humoured me over the years while
I have bored them stiff with talk and snippets as
this piece has come together.

Thanks to all the patients and others who
have knowingly or inadvertently inspired
90% of the raw material.

And thanks to those unknown, whose gags have been
recycled in some form. Where appropriate, OMG –
Old Medical Gags – alerts appear in the text. Well,
they say recycling is good for the environment. If the
originators are (i) still alive and/or (ii) brave enough
to 'fess up, I should be delighted to acknowledge
their valuable contributions.

Ray Leonardsson, May 2(

Preface

OK, to the best of my knowledge, fish do not as a rule suffer from diabetes mellitus. The reason behind the title, however, will become clear later in the book.

'Who's the Diabetic Fish?' follows the action on a 'long day shift' in the emergency admissions ward of a general hospital. As a nurse, I have seen many incidents and had experiences that are the basis for this work. Many real situations have been more amusing than made-up gags, and are reflected in the sanity-preserving occupational 'gallows' humour, but with a genuine affection for the job, my colleagues, (most of) my patients, and with the greatest respect for the nursing profession in general. And there are more old gags than you can shake a stick at, so please cut me some slack. Advance warning of the most criminal of these is given at relevant places in the text.

At its heart, 'Who's the Diabetic Fish?' is a tribute to the front line, the infantry of the NHS, the 'neat-plain-black-shoes, hair-neatly-tied-back, small-discreet-stud-earrings, nails-kept-short' brigade, the sloggers, the people who care from the guts outward, and turn up day after day to care for fellow human beings – to give a damn. Because, in essence, nursing is just that, and is very simple – one human being caring for another. If you feel mildly satirised, please bear with me. I still love, honour, and (occasionally) obey you.

This is a work of fiction, although I estimate I have seen over 90% of the content in real life, and some of the situations and conversations have seemed totally bizarre. How do you wrap up a cup of tea, for example? Where real events have inspired the piece, there has been anonymisation, combination, and minor caricature to protect the innocent (and sometimes the guilty).

This started life as a musical work. Since the songs are a vital part of the narrative, I have left them in. All but two of the lyrics ('Blues' and 'Ethanol Rap') are inspired by tunes of popular songs. Feel free to sing along (best option) or just read, if you'd rather. Who can forget the Village People-inspired 'MRSA', the Abba-themed 'Thank You for Me New Hip', or the timeless Queen-like classic 'Bohospital Rhapsody'? If you are unfamiliar with some of the suggested tunes, you may find it useful to have your preferred music streaming service to hand.

Caution:

Made with material from more than one hospital. Contains vernacular references to body parts and the fluids thereof, and one or two cases of mild bad language. No nurses were harmed in the writing of this book, but some of them will never be quite the same again. May contain nuts. Look away to avoid flashing images.

The Long Day
(Twelve-and-a-half hours)

Songs

Inspired by the tunes of popular songs (except 'Blues' and 'Ethanol Rap', which are left to your imagination)

1. Prologue

I don't remember that calorie from yesterday, thought Lucy, catching the mirror as she barrelled across the landing en route to the shower, past her twins' bedroom. 'Boys, get up – dropping you off at Nan's in 15 minutes.'

The squeal of the cat signified the probable loss of one life. 'Should have been quicker there,' mused Mitzy later, licking her squashed tail. 'That's five left.'

A quick splash, a jump into some clothes, and Lucy was ready. But why are toddlers so slow when you're running late? 'Hurry up, you two!' she snapped, nearly smudging her lippy. Then, one twin on each arm, bag handle between her teeth, off to her mum's, a 'see you later' peck for the boys, and straight out into the roadworks and behind a broken-down lorry. 'Hope it's not going to be one of those days.'

Hospital, just before dawn. Bay 4. Emergency Medical Ward. Everything appears settled and calm; just the occasional lowing sound from the sleeping occupants of the six beds. But things are about to change. Someone is waking in the corner. He sits up slowly and slips out of bed, starting to make his way across the bay to the bed opposite. But wait... is that a catheter bag still hooked onto the bed frame? ...stretching... stretching... creak... This could hurt.

Oblivious to the restful environment, Arthur lets out a piercing shriek that would make a statue wince and shed a tear, as the balloon end of the catheter is pulled roughly against its will down his urethra, and explodes into the outside world with a twanging, slapping, 'boing!' sound – well, you can read how difficult it is to describe. Safe to say, the exit was not without discomfort.

So much for a gentle awakening. 'Woss going on?' 'Who's making that noise?' Norman, in the middle bed, sits up, fiddling with the line in his arm, inevitably pulling his cannula out and setting the drip alarm off as he starts to bleed, trailing red droplets across the floor as he tries to find his way to the toilet in the dim light.

Gerald and Chris stumble out of bed – one with his Zimmer frame in an approximation of support – and disturb the other two occupants. Just in case they were trying to have a lie-in, perhaps? The noise level rises along with the level of confusion, escalating into mayhem as drip stands fall, Zimmer frames topple, and call buttons are set off.

Two of the night staff rush to the bay and try to bring some calm, separating two patients engaged in meaningless unarmed combat. Arthur spots them.

'Oi! Who are you? Come in 'ere, spoiling our fight! Just 'cos you're wearing a uniform! Piss off!'

Another day begins.

2. Handover

With Arthur's new catheter safely inserted, gradually calm was restored, as the day shift arrived for another routinely unpredictable day. Handover gave them some sort of a rough idea what to expect.

'What a night. The shift from hell!'

'Are you back again tonight?' Brian enquired sympathetically of the night nurse.

'No, but if I was, I wouldn't be.'

'OK, let's get on so you can get home to bed.'

'Side Ward 1 – 82-year-old gentleman. Lives alone. Daughter next of kin. Found on the floor by neighbour – probably been there all night. Dysphasic and confused. Difficult to get a good history, but his daughter says he has had mini strokes in the past, and she's not sure he's coping very well on his own. He's been seen by the doctor and had all his routine blood tests, ECG, and chest X-ray. Hourly obs. Intravenous infusion in situ with one litre of normal saline running over eight hours. Catheterised on hourly measurement. Urine dipped, sample sent. Card out for CT head scan, probably tomorrow. Bay 1, Bed 1 – One hundred and eleven.'

'Really, that old?' Brian raised his eyebrows.

'Oh sorry, my writing. He's *ill*. Incompetent of urine.'

Becky questioned, 'Don't you mean incontinent?'

'No. He can use a bottle, but misses most of the time.

Bed 2 – Social admission, in here while his house is being decorated. Mobile, self-neglecting.

Bed 3 – Olympic furtler – and thinks next door's locker is his own private bathroom.

Bed 4 – Empty – self-discharged; took exception to bed 3 using his locker as his own private bathroom.

Bed 5 – Undercover reporter from *The Sun*. Written up for oral, intravenous and per rectal Domestos four times a day – just to make sure he doesn't catch anything he can put on the front page.'

Brian jumped in, 'Can I do the PR?'

'No, Brian, it's my turn. You did the bloke from the *Daily Mail* last week.' Becky liked fairness.

'I'm sure you can sort that out between yourselves.

Bed 6 – Watch him. Nicks anything he can get his hands on.'

'Is that evidence-based?' Brian was a stickler for best practice.

'Yes. Saw him on *Crimewatch* last week.'

The second night nurse took up the story. 'Bay 2, Bed 1 – Nothing wrong with her, but likes to wear her nightie all the time. Being in hospital it helps her feel poorly.'

'Ah, bless!' the day shift responded in unison.

'Bed 2 – This is the lady with chronic polyproctalgia.'

Becky had picked up a few Greek syllables from one of the junior doctors.

'That's the persistent pain in the—'

'Exactly. If she went to the Chelsea Flower Show, she'd moan there were too many plants. Nothing much wrong with her – burn to her ear. Phone went while she was ironing. Bed 3 – Don't really know why she's here; NHS 111 sent her. Something about she's run out of grapes and Sainsbury's was closed. Bed 4 – Just in for the weekend. GP doesn't do home visits after Friday lunch. Having said that, we think she might have diabetes. Awaiting test results. Bed 5 – A bit agitated. Hasn't really cottoned on to where she is. Possibly a bit of post-traumatic stress. She recently got stranded in IKEA for a week. Couldn't find her way out.'

'Is she mobile?'

'Oh, yes, mobilises well from bed to floor.'

'Did you put an incident form in?'

'You bet I did. Completely ruined my break, she did. Bed 6 – Stop all her medication.'

'Why, is she better?' Becky again.

'No. The lady in the bed opposite likes to share. Throws hers across. Side ward – Good news or bad news?'

'Good news.'

'She's formed a beneficial therapeutic, holistic relationship.'

'And the bad news?'

'With the fairies.'

'Ah, bless!' the day shift responded in unison (again).

'Oh, and her feeding tube is out. Bit of Yorkshire got stuck. And finally, the other side room. 101-year-old lady came in with chest pain. History of heart failure. Has been referred to the archaeologist. Sorry, slip of the tongue. Cardiologist. And that's about it.'

'So, how was the shift?' Becky enquired cautiously.

'Hectic or what? Patients, doctors, audits for everything that moves – and things that don't – targets, attitude surveys, more audits, training, upcoming meetings, BPs, IVs, DVTs, D&V, PRs, GPs, HVs, IPC, plans of care...'

'Driving you spare?'

'Yeah. Then relatives and sedatives, enemas, BMs, DNs, INRs, DNRs, CQC, CCG... oh, and the new efficiency drive. We've all got to increase productivity by 25%. That reminds me, must dash, or I'll miss my operation.'

'What operation?'

'I'm having a surgical implant.'

'Silicon?'

'No, broom. And there's talk about being fitted with catheters and drips soon, so we don't waste time having breaks. Oh, and before you start, the infection control nurse wants a word.'

The infection control nurse sashayed in, spraying disinfectant from a small aerosol. She addressed the assembled company.

'Now, remember when you were little, your mummies and daddies told you to always wash your hands when you went to the toilet, and before your dinner? Well, it's a bit like that, except you need to wash your hands when anyone *else* goes to the toilet or has their dinner.'

Brian slid the words out of the corner of his mouth. 'Why not go the whole hog and call it "din-dins"?'

The indignant response was instant. 'Because you're all grown-ups now. Anyway, I've got a little song to help you remember to wash your hands. All stand up now, because there are some actions. Research has shown...'

Brian feigned a yawn. 'Just get on with it.'

'Off we go then. All standing up? One, two, three…'

Tune: Traditional children's song.

If you're dirty and you know it, wash your hands.
If you're dirty and you know it, wash your hands.
If you're dirty and you know it, but you
do not want to show it,
If you're dirty and you know it, wash your hands.

In a vain attempt to engender some enthusiasm, the visitor interjected. 'Come on now, all of you, I want to see you all doing the actions!' Obstinate zero response.

If you cannot see the dirt, then use the gel,
If you cannot see the dirt then use the gel,
If you do not use the gel, you will surely go to hell,
If you cannot see the dirt, then use the gel.

We don't want any germs surviving here,
We don't want any germs surviving here.
If no germs survive in here,
There's no sick and diarrhoea,
So we don't want any germs surviving here.

We want this place to be so squeaky clean,
We want this place to be so squeaky clean.
To be so squeaky clean that
We won't know where you've been,
We want this place to be so squeaky clean.

3. General Duties

Sister Karen spoke for them all. 'So, now we know, children. Shall we get to work? Bed washes.'

'Shall I get the hosepipe, Sister?' Student Nurse Nicole was keen to start her placement by making a good impression.

'Touchingly traditional, my dear, but we do things differently now – one at a time,' Sister Karen responded without a hint of condescension.

And so the day began in earnest, with the general bustle of washing, drug rounds, people carrying bowls and wheeling rattling linen trollies all over the place. Why, oh why, had nobody devised a wheeled medical device that did not squeak and squeal like a busy night on *Springwatch*? Perhaps a little irreverently, several staff moved about in time with the hand-washing song, the words gently wafting in the breeze. Was there a hint of a tap dance as Becky strode about her business?

Lucy rushed in, breathless, with a makeshift bandage round her head.

'Sorry I'm late, Sister.'

Lucy had a heart of gold, but Karen was used to her bohemian timekeeping.

'What was it this time? Oversleep? Hamster poorly? Wrong sort of milk on your muesli? Trouble parking your broomstick? And what's the bandage for?'

'Texting. Walked into a lamppost. Shall I just get on? Mr Ellis needs a shave.'

'Better cross-match him for two units of blood then,' chuckled Karen. She had experience of NHS razors.

A small kerfuffle in the corridor. A care assistant had slopped a few drops of water, alerting an eagle-eyed cleanliness technician, who had dashed on with her mop and trolley, complete with bright yellow cones, which she distributed with relish. '**Beware of Spillages**' they boldly proclaimed. Their arrival was followed by another cleanliness technician with more cones to trump those of her colleague – '**Beware of Cones – Trip Hazard**'.

Leanne, the Health Care Assistant and progenitor of the incident, wryly observed, 'I couldn't be a domestic. Wouldn't know which colour bucket to use.'

The early bustle resumed, with staff simply veering round the cones. A minor inconvenience, nothing more. Meanwhile, Becky was into her drug round.

'Hello, Janet. I've got your injection.'

'Thank you, nurse. It's my birthday today as well.'

'Congratulations. Not often you get poked with a sharp object on your birthday, is it?'

'I'M NOT TELLING YOU!' retorted Janet, with just a hint of a twinkle in her eye.

Becky moved swiftly on. 'Hello, Gerald. Your Viagra. Just a quarter of a tablet, wasn't it?'

'That's right. Thank you.'

Student Nicole looked perplexed. 'That was a bit strange. Why is he only on a quarter? I thought you had to take the whole dose of a drug to get the full effect.'

'Oh, his wife was fed up of him dribbling on his slippers. Let's move on, shall we? Norman, do you take any regular medication?'

'No.' Long pause. 'Just tablets.'

'What tablets do you take then, Norman?'

'White ones.'

'That narrows it down a bit. OK. Let's try a different angle. What do you take them for?'

'Doctor told me to.'

Becky tried unsuccessfully not to appear exasperated. 'Tell you what, here are the keys to the trolley. If you see anything you recognise, just help yourself.'

Meanwhile, enter the phlebotomist. Noticing Brian in the bay out of the corner of her eye, she approached the patient opposite.

'Hello, you're Chris, aren't you? I've come to take some blood.'

'Oh, so you're the vampire, are you?'

The blood-taker rolled her eyes to the ceiling in a 'for goodness sake' sort of way. 'If I had a pound for every time I've heard that... just a little prick.'

Brian was suddenly aware of her presence. 'You said you wouldn't tell anyone! Wait till I get you home...'

'Your home or mine?'

These little flirtations, never sinister, helped the day go by, although these days you had to watch your Ps and Qs in case you upset someone.

Chloe and Leanne, the HCAs, pulled the curtain round Gerald's bed.

'Now, Gerald, we'd just like to check your pressure areas... Mmm. They look ok. We don't want you to develop any sore bits. Now, we just need to reposition your bottom.'

Gerald fancied himself as a bit of a wit. 'What are you going to do? Move it round to the front?'

'Can't do that,' said Leanne earnestly. ''elf 'n' safety.'

Oh well...

4. Ward Round

WARNING: This chapter contains more than its fair share of OMGs[*]. You may wish to carry out alternative pursuits for its duration. For example, climb the North Face of the Eiger in flip-flops, or perhaps navigate Cape Horn in a coracle. Or just bite on a (clean) rolled-up hanky and read on.

While the daily care went on around her, Sister Karen greeted Dr Rock, the consultant, and his junior, Dr Roe. Karen thought it was a shame he was not called Dr Roll. Rock and Roll would have had a certain... She abruptly abandoned her reverie.

'Good morning, Dr Rock, Dr Roe.'

Brian emerged from the bay as they arrived.

'You don't want to go in there. They're all mad as badgers.'

'That's unfair to badgers,' Karen retorted, without thinking. *What was she on this morning?* 'I should report you. As a matter of fact, I collect badgers.'

'Really?'

'Yes. I've nearly got the sett,' she replied, surprising herself, and suppressing a little chuckle.

'Harrumph. Good morning, Sister. Shall we press on?'

The consultant marched in a business-like manner to the first bed. 'Now what's the problem here?'

---

[*] Old Medical Gags

Ted put on as poorly a face as he could muster. 'Doctor, I get this dreadful pain when I cough.'

'Hmm... well, just stop coughing.'

'No, Doctor, you don't understand. I'm having trouble getting my breath.'

Suggested tune: (I can't get no) *Satisfaction* – Rolling Stones

> *I can't get my respiration.*
> *Pain is worse on inspiration,*
> *But I try (cough), yes, I try (cough+),*
> *Yes, I try (cough++)*
> *How I try (cough & gasp+++.)*
> *I can't get my respiration.*

> *I was coughing down the road,*
> *So I went along to my GP.*
> *He said, 'I think you have COPD*
> *Coz you've got a wheeze. Now I can see*
> *Your lungs are half the size they used to be.'*

Dr Rock was not slow to pick up the gist.

> *You can't get your respiration...*
> *What you've got is inflammation...*

> *You can't walk and you gasp for breath,*
> *Pretty soon you will be close to death.*
> *What you need, it's urgent, man,*
> *Is an X-ray and a CT scan.*

> *Now I want you to take a nebuliser,*
> *But that is just the appetiser,*

Coz you'll never make it on your own.
You need steroids – prednisolone, or you won't have
no Respiration, no respiration, no respiration (fade)

'Ok. Let's get you an X-ray and I'll look at it later. We'll give it our best, old chap. Meanwhile, keep your oxygen on. Blue is SO not your colour.'

'Thank you. Doctor.'

'Who's next, Sister?'

'This patient is unable to get out of bed, Doctor. Thinks he's broken his leg. We're waiting for his X-ray to be reviewed.'

Gerald, the wit, seized his opportunity. 'I've been here so long they sent me a payslip last week.'

Unimpressed, Dr Rock examined the X-ray carefully. 'That looks fine. Nothing wrong there.'

Gerald, mistakenly fancying he was on a bit of a roll, put his glasses on. 'Sorry, what was that? Couldn't hear you without my glasses on.'

Dr Rock was not going to rise to the bait. Louder and slowly, he intoned, 'THERE'S NOTHING WRONG WITH YOU!'

'Oh great! Thanks, Doc.' Gerald leapt out of the bed and ran off, never to be seen again.

'Ah, the power of the curative X-ray. What's the matter with the next chap?'

'He's depressed, Doctor.'

'Good morning, Mr er…'

Mr Er, or Chris – as his friends and family called him – sullenly uttered his rejoinder. 'What's good about it?'

'What seems to be the matter? How are you today?'

Tune: Blues – improvise as you see fit, dear reader.

> *Woke up this morning*
> *Ooohh I was feeling bad. (pause)*
> *Then I got worse.*
> *Life is just driving me mad.*

'So, what happened to you?' Dr Rock duly engaged his patient with an open question.

> *Weee…eeell, my baby left me,*
> *My dog died, and I turned to drink.*
> *Lost my job, my roof fell in.*
> *Just need some time to think.*

'And then…' Dr Rock gave him permission to continue.

> *So I went to make some tea,*
> *And the kettle boiled dry.*
> *The milk was curdled,*
> *I just wanted to cry.*

'Erm…' Dr Rock held back a tear as Chris ploughed on.

> *Then my telly broke down*
> *In the middle of the England game.*
> *Missed the goal and the second half,*
> *Then knock at the door and the bailiffs came.*

'Mmm. OK. So you've really had a rough time latel—'

> *Oh, ooohhh, ooohhh yeah!*
> *Life couldn't be worse,*

Feel I'm under a curse,
I don't understand it.
My life just feels like sh—

With a timely interruption, Dr Rock summarised, 'Ok. I'm starting to get a pattern here. Let's see…'

Just don't know how to cope.
Life's rotten – haven't got any hope,
I feel so-ooo-ooo-oooo bad
It's driving me maa-aaaa-aaaad.

Almost, but not quite under his breath, Dr Rock expressed his thoughts frankly. 'I think you're driving us all mad.' Then to the patient, 'Ok. Ok. I get the picture.'

Brian, trying to help, put his two-pennyworth in. 'If he was a horse, we'd have to shoot him.'

A lightbulb seemed to go on inside Dr Rock's head.

'Hold on, that gives me an idea. I know just the thing for you, old chap. Draw the curtain, Nurse.'

The crack of the gunshot silenced everyone for a moment, startled.

'Thanks, Doctor, that's better. Much better.'

Thud. The sound drew Lucy to the bay. 'Brian, what was that?'

'Particularly bad case of Bodkin Adams Prognosis.'

Dr Rock was in no mood to drag out his ward round. 'Now, who's next?' he mouthed. 'Ah yes. Let's see the colonoscopy report. Mmm… What's this?'

Brian, ever helpful, turned the print the right way up. The question was rhetorical, but Brian answered it anyway. 'It's an arse, Doctor.'

'I KNOW that. I AM an arse doctor!' the consultant retorted tetchily, before turning to the patient. 'Now, what appears to be the matter?'

'Doctor, I have a problem with my bowels – I move them every morning at six-thirty on the dot,' Norman answered.

'That's not a problem, is it?'

'Well, yes, it is really, Doctor. I don't get up until eight.'

'When did you discover you had this trouble?'

'When I took my bed socks off.'

'Right. We'll need a specimen, Nurse.'

Brian turned to the passing care assistant. 'Could you do that please, Leanne?'

'Nah. 'elf 'n' safety.'

Nonetheless, Dr Rock requested again (tunefully).

Serving suggestion: *Catch a Falling Star* – Perry Como

Catch a falling faece and put it in a bottle
Send it to the lab today.
If it shows up C-Diff,
You will need some treatment
In an isolation bay.

We'll put you in a side room – don't feel you're rejected
'Cos you're being shut away.
We have to be sure that others aren't infected –
We'll look in on you twice a day.

'Moving swiftly on then. Who is next?'

'Mr White-Lightning, Doctor.' Karen lowered her voice, 'A bit of a drinker.'

'Yes, I can see that. Looks like a traffic light without the red and green. Good morning.'

'Good morning, Doctor,' said Arthur surprisingly chirpily, given his parlous state of health.

'I'm Doctor Rock.'

Tune: Rap. Again, dear reader, improvise as you see fit.

You've come here, bin drinkin' beer
For many years, now the tears. You not so mellow,
Turning yellow, sorry, fellow, jaundice yellow.
You're not so hot, liver's shot, started to rot,

Your blood won't clot, You're down a hole,
no bowel control, soakin' wet, incontinent.

Not so fine, drinkin' wine, beer an' cider, all the time,
Chardonnay, Beaujolais, Merlot, Cabernet, Rose,
Every day in quantity and you don't see
It ain't no tonic, you're alcoholic.

You don't know the side effects,

Never know what's comin' next,
You ain't havin' no more sex,
'Cos your partner's now your ex,
So no more sex, just Pabrinex.

So LFTs, U&Es, banding for your varices,
GI bleed so NG feed,
Try to get it fixed.

Arthur suddenly looked anxious. 'Doctor, couldn't you just give me something for my liver?'

Dr Roe was feeling a bit left out, so it was a relief when Dr Rock turned to him.

'Write him up for a pound of onions, please, Dr Roe.'

Dr Rock moved on. 'Now, this next gentleman doesn't look very ill.'

'It's not me, Doctor. My wife thinks she's a chicken.'

'How long has this been going on?'

'About eighteen months.'

'Why didn't you come in earlier?'

'We needed the eggs.'

Dr Rock bristled and muttered – at the same time, 'Oh dear. Give me strength.'

He offered John what he considered sound advice. 'Don't give up the day job, old chap. Now, please leave the space you are in to somebody who needs it. Good day to you. Now, the lady in the side room, Sister.'

'And what's brought you in here?'

'A fish bone stuck in my throat and I choked, Doctor.'

'Was it cod or haddock?'

'Turbot.'

'Oh, far too posh for the NHS, my dear. Did you consider going private? Nurse, arrange to transfer this patient to the Nuffield. I'll see her in my clinic there. I think that's it, Sister. I'll be back later to review the test results.'

Dr Rock left the ward, musing on the unconventional cure he had just administered. To secure his place in history, he really needed a condition or syndrome to his name. Barrett had his oesophagus, Bell his palsy, and even surgeons were in on the act. Archie McIndoe had his forceps, and Hartmann both a fluid *and* a procedure. Sadly, Ehlers and Danlos shared 13 versions of their syndrome. One would have been harsh enough, but 13 was truly heart-breaking.

He reflected for a moment. The list of those who had left their names to posterity – de la Tourette, Parkinson, Hodgkin and his cousin Non, Crohn, Klinefelter; it was almost endless. Even Q (probably not the James Bond one) had his sign. But not Rock. Not yet. He needed something, but with more gravitas than 'Rock's Rectum'. He spared a thought for the diligent folk from Bristol, who he felt had been given a raw deal. The dirty end of the stick, if you like. For no particular reason, he smiled to himself.

5. Pharmacist, A Phone Call, and a Scan

'Good morning, Norman. I'm the pharmacist. I've just come to check your medication.'

Cheery tune: *My Favourite Things* - from *The Sound of Music*

Capsules and potions with various lotions,
Numerous liquids to stimulate motions,
Bright coloured tablets to cure all your ills –
This is my business, I do it with pills.

Nasty discharges that come from your penis, (or for
those of a sensitive disposition 'if you have an illness
that's really quite heinous'),
We could consider something intravenous.
But don't expect it to work in a day –
May be some weeks till you're ready to play.

When the bugs bite, when the pain strikes,
When you're feeling bad:
Just take all the tablets that I give to you,
And soon you'll be feeling glad.

Blood pressure, heartburn, or new diabetes,
Weeing too often or arthritic kneesies,
Here in my book I have something for you,
To make you feel better or help you to poo.

Gout, or nausea, deep depression,
We've a pill for you.
If you have a headache, paracetamol
Will do the job well – take two.

Isosorbide mononitrate – once or twice a day,
If you've got angina it's going to help
To take any pain away.

Meanwhile, at the hospital switchboard...

Ring. Ring ring. Ring ring. Ring ring. Ring ring. Ring ring. Ring ring. Ring ring. Ring ring. Ring ring. Ring ring.

'Hello, District Hospital. How may I help you?'

'Hello. I'm phoning about Mrs. Tiptree. She has been with you several days and I'm concerned about her. How is she doing, and will she be going home soon? I've been very worried.'

'One moment, I'll put you through to the ward.'

Ring ring. Ring ring. Ring ring. Ring ring. Ring ring. Ring ring. Ring ring. Ring ring. Ring ring. Ring ring. Ring ring.

'Hello, Emergency Admissions. Ward clerk speaking. How may I help you?'

'Hello. I'm phoning about Mrs. Tiptree. She has been with you several days and I'm concerned about her. How is she doing, and will she be going home soon? I've been very worried.'

'One moment, I'll put you through to the nurses' station.'

Ring ring. Ring ring. Ring ring. Ring ring. Ring ring. Ring ring. Ring ring. Ring ring. Ring ring. Ring ring. Ring ring. Ring ring.

'Hello, nurses' station. Staff Nurse Becky speaking. How may I help you?'

'Hello. I'm phoning about Mrs. Tiptree. She has been with you several days and I'm concerned about her. How is she doing, and will she be going home soon? I've been very worried.'

'One moment, I'll find the nurse who's looking after her, and get her to have a word with you.'

There was a long pause while Becky located Lucy, who then had to disgorge herself from her patient, take off her apron and gloves, wash her hands, answer a call bell en route to the phone, and get to the nurses' station.

'Hello, Staff Nurse Lucy. How may I help you?'

'Hello. I'm phoning about Mrs. Tiptree. She has been with you several days and I'm concerned about her. How is she doing, and will she be going home soon? I've been very worried.'

'Just one moment, I'll check the notes.'

First of all, thought Lucy, looking at the space where the notes trolley resided on occasions, *find the notes*. A grand tour of the ward finally revealed the trolley where it had been left after the ward round.

That's my ten thousand steps for today, anyway, thought Lucy as she got back to the phone.

'Hello, sorry to keep you waiting. Could you just confirm what you are calling about?'

'Yes. I'm phoning about Mrs. Tiptree. She has been with you several days and I'm concerned about her. How is she doing, and will she be going home soon? I've been very worried.'

'Well, I've checked the notes. She seems to be getting better. Her diarrhoea has settled, the physiotherapists are happy with her, and she is eating and drinking well. She is due for a blood test tomorrow, and if that is clear, we should be able to send her home.'

'That is good news. I've been very worried.'

'You do sound worried. Are you a friend or relative?'

'No. I'm Mrs. Tiptree. No-one tells me bugger all around here.'

Becky was still busying herself among her patients. She always tried to have time to chat to them, however busy she may have been with all the routine 'nursie' stuff. 'How are you today, Elsie?'

'I've never been on a boat like this before.'

'Boat?' Becky smiled. 'This is a bed.'

'Don't be silly. A bed would sink before it got out of the harbour.'

'You're not in the harbour, Elsie. You're in hospital.'

'Don't be so silly. Why would I be in hospital on this boat?'

'You're not on a boat. This is a hospital bed. It might feel a bit wavy because it's an air mattress – to stop your bottom getting sore.'

'Piffle. I was in the Navy, you know. Wrens, they called us.'

Becky thought for a moment, and decided to go with the flow, dipping her toe into the patient's world. Odd place to dip a toe, but here goes…

'Did you go to sea?'

'Oh yes. Those were the days. There weren't many of us girls then, you know.' Elsie paused, wistfully recalling memories of the times she obviously cherished; times that were special to her. 'Oh yes, I've shipped my fair share of captains in my time.'

'Don't you mean captained a lot of ships?' Becky attempted to correct her.

With the wickedest of winks and an obvious twinkle appearing in her eye, Elsie was suddenly alert and in the zone.

'I know what I mean, dear. Up with the lark, to bed with the Wren, they used to say. I could tell you things to make your hair curl,' she almost cackled.

'Sounds like you could certainly tell me a few tales, Elsie. Do you know where you are?'

'Yes. I'm on this lovely boat in the harbour.'

'Would you like to go on a short voyage?' Becky stayed in the moment.

'Where to?'

'We'd like to take you for a scan. You'll go on your bed… er, boat.'

'Escan. Sounds nice there.'

'Would you like your cup of tea and biscuit before you go?'

'No. Wrap it up for me. I'll have it when I return from foreign parts.'

While Becky was weighing up the technicalities of wrapping up a cup of tea, the X-ray staff arrived to take Elsie for her CT scan.

'Do you know where you are, Elsie?' *One more try*, Becky thought.

'Of course. I'm going for a scan. And whatever made you think I was on a boat? I'm in hospital, on a bed.' Elsie sighed as she was wheeled off the ward toward the lift. 'Silly girl.'

Later, Becky reflected on her day, and on that little incident in particular. Her patients were not just medical conditions or in need of health or social interventions. (*How impersonal a word is 'intervention'?* she mused.) Her patients, like Elsie and many others, were real people who had had (and were still having) lives and experiences. Wherever they came from, whatever they'd made of their lives, each one was uniquely experienced; each one had their own story to tell, of singular experiences that had brought them to where they were – physically, mentally, emotionally, spiritually. They had families, loved ones they had inspired, been role models, achievers, contributors, all in their own ways – probably still were, in one form or another.

Their experience of her care would impact differently on every one of them, and add to their treasury of memories, even if the mechanics of their care were similar. Her role and that of her colleagues (who also had lives outside and stories to tell) was to be part of that journey, however short the encounter, and to contribute to the worthwhileness and purpose of that journey, even if it was the final instalment. *Never forget that*, she told herself, concluding that dementia and ill health were levellers and thieves in equal measure. Everyone she looked after was in her care for one reason. They were poorly, full stop; just as convicts were in prison for one reason – they got nicked. Heroin addict or aristocrat (or both). All poorly. Some would be content with their lot through life; others would be bearing the scars of bitter experience; some would be shocked to the marrow with their current dependent state and possibly embarrassed at their present situation. But not a single one of them would suffer that embarrassment nor any indignity. Not on Becky's watch. Humility is what you do to yourself first so that others will not feel humiliated, even when being afforded the most intimate care.

6. Physiotherapy

Look out, physios on the ward! Time for the patients' workouts. And don't forget the Occupational Therapists. It was time to think about getting folk home and coping as well as they could with a bit of support and help.

Advice for performing: *Saturday Night's Alright for Fighting* – Elton John. You may like to play along on your air guitar, identifying with patients who need support as you cavort with jerky movements at gravity-defying angles. Avoid trying to sing this one in the bath.

Physio, physio, physio, physio, physiotherapy,
Physio, physio, physio, physio, physiotherapy.

We've come to get you out today,
Time to get up off your bed;
Rehabilitation starts today,
'coz that's what the doctor said.
Sitting out from bed to chair,
We'll start in such a simple way,
Then we'll walk out with a Zimmer frame –
Do a little more each day.

Oh, oohh… we want to get you independent,
So that you can cope at home,
Someone to help with shopping, cleaning,
Visit you when you're alone.

We'll have a chat with the dietitian,
Making sure you're eating well.
And just in case you've fallen over,
We'll sort a pendant alar-ar-arm be-e-ll, be-e-e-ell.

We're here to help you get about,
Getting up and down the stairs,
Reducing hazards in your house,
Don't want you taken unawares;
So you can bath and use the kitchen,
So that you can wash and cook,
Maybe you need loo seat-raiser,
We'll pop around and take a look.

A kitchen test is quite essential,
See you make a cup of tea,
And then an Age UK befriender,
'cos you've got no family.

Oh ooohh, we want to get you independent...

Physio, physio, physio, physio, physio...

A physiotherapist had just taken Janet onto the stairs for what was called, unsurprisingly, a 'stairs assessment' before she went home. She pronounced her fit for discharge and Janet could not hide her delight.

Feelgood singalong melody: *Thank You for the Music – Abba*

Walking around was becoming a bit of a chore,
And every so often I had to be scraped off the floor.

Then I met a surgeon who said, 'Get a grip!
In a matter of hours I can make you a hip
With titanium in';
So I threw my old hip in the bin.

Now I say
Thank you for me new hip,
My life was minging,
Now it's great, my legs are swinging.
Can't believe the difference, I say in all honesty,
I feel so free,
I got my Zimmer and threw it away.
So I say thank you for me new hip, for giving it to me.

I feel so healthy with my new bionic hip
I want to show the world I can do leapfrog –
I can hop, I can run, I can skip.

So I say thank you for me new hip,
My life was minging,
Now it's great, my legs are swinging.
Can't believe the difference, I say in all honesty,
I feel so free,
I got my Zimmer and threw it away.
So I say thank you for me new hip, for giving it to me.

7. Lunchtime/Visiting

The meal trolley trundled noisily onto the ward, announcing its arrival in advance. The housekeeper rang the bell to summon her troop of lunch deliverers and feeding assistants, and set to issuing green aprons before turning her attention to the trayed meals in the trolley.

She pulled the first one out. 'Who's the diabetic fish?'

Chloe intervened. 'I didn't think fish could get diabetes. But Brenda has diabetes and has ordered the fish, if that's what you mean.'

Chloe went about her business, turning her attention to Ted.

'What's this?' he enquired, looking at the tray in front of him.

'It's bean casserole.'

Ted's retort was straight out of the 'Pan Book of Very Old and Familiar Hospital Gags'.

'I didn't ask what it had been. What is it now? Have you got anything else?'

Housekeeper to the rescue. 'We've got tuna mayonnaise sandwiches – oh, wait a minute, what does it say here? Ohh... Not your ordinary tuna mayonnaise, but POLE AND LINE CAUGHT tuna mayonnaise. Must be our new eco-friendly gourmet range. Do you know what that means? Let me explain. In order to catch the fish for this sandwich, they used a FISHING ROD! Not just a rod – I suppose it's difficult getting close enough to a tuna to pat it on the head – but a pole AND a line. How they caught the mayonnaise remains a mystery. Perhaps they got a bit on the end of the pole.'

Ted was not that impressed by this apparent aspiration to Michelin stardom, but he was hungry.

'Sounds as pretentious as *MasterChef*, but basically ethical. I'll have one of those. Thank you.'

*

The clock ticked, although nobody could hear it. Perhaps it was electric. Gradually, visitors started to gather outside the door, as if waiting for the opening of the January sales. Sister Karen opened the door and unleashed the usual tsunami of friends and relatives – some desperate to see loved ones, some doing their duty, some just in it for the chocolate and the grapes. When the flood subsided to a steady trickle, one stern-looking woman entered with clipboard and pencil and sat down in a forthright manner beside the bed containing her mother. Then one large shaven-headed primate of a man belligerently approached the nurses' station.

'Oi, you just sittin' there puttin' yer lippy on, or are you lookin' after me mum?'

Brian was startled and resented the implications of the remark, but composed himself.

'Can't say I wear a lot of lipstick. Sorry, how can I help you?'

'Me mum. When's she comin' 'ome?'

'What's your mother's name?'

'Don't yer know? You're meant to be lookin' after 'er. Bleedin' useless. 'ave to go 'ome and get me own bleedin' dinner now I 'spose. Again.' He stomped out, knuckles almost rubbing on the ground.

'Perhaps if I'd found out who *he* was, I could have found out who his mother was,' Brian mused, but not quite under his breath.

The stern woman with clipboard duly made a note. A haughty man, smartly dressed, approached. Brian surmised that his vehicle of choice might be a BMW.

'My grandmother was brought in here yesterday. Had a fall. Er, name of Hawkins. Elsie Hawkins. I'm her grandson, Justin Hawkins. I hope you're looking after her properly. If anything happens to her...'

'She's comfortable today. Had a good night. Went for a scan this morning. We're waiting for the report.'

'Why has she only just been for it? I want you to fix her. Don't want her getting any of those bugs. I work for a claims solicitor, you know.'

Retro time: *Take Good Care of My Baby* – Bobby Vee

Take good care of my granny
She's not feeling very well.
She had a fall last Sunday,
We found her late on Monday
We think she must have been through hell.

I'm a member of the public
And I insist you fix my gran.
If she does not get better,
Then there will be a letter
To my MP and your top man.

33

That little gran's a treasure
We'd really miss her so.
We love her without measure,
We saw her just a year ago.

So take good care of my granny,
Don't you dare to let her fall.
And if you should discover
That she will not recover,
Then I'll come back again and sue you all.

Chloe was watching. 'What was that about?'

'Compensation vulture circulating. Works for an ambulance-chasing parasite,' Brian replied. An idea forced itself upon him at the thought of someone eyeing up the prospect of getting an out-of-court financial settlement from the NHS. He turned to haughty Hawkins.

'Excuse me, would you mind if I head-butted you? There are risks of bodily injury with this procedure.'

'No, not at all. Go ahead. Make my day.'

Sarky, eh? Perfect. Brian took his chance with relish. Despite the early warning, the element of surprise worked a treat.

'Oi, you're not allowed to do that!'

'Yes, I am. You gave me your informed consent.'

The stern woman made another little note. Another lady approached the nurses' station and addressed Brian.

'Nothing personal, but do you have a female nurse I could speak to, please?'

'Certainly. I'll find one of my colleagues for you.'

Becky arrived.

'Sorry to bother you, but I'm just visiting my auntie. While I'm here, would it be possible to get some contraception?'

'Not really. You need to see your GP clinic.'

'But I can't get an appointment today. Could I just have a word with a doctor?'

Dr Roe happened to be checking some blood results. 'Sorry, not much we can do here, I'm afraid.'

'Oh dear. I'm really quite desperate. I'm planning to have sexual intercourse this evening.'

'All I can suggest is that you have some paracetamol,' Dr Roe replied, trying to appear helpful.

'That's not contraception, is it? And I haven't got a headache.'

Shouldn't get in the way of her plans for tonight then, thought Doctor Roe, whilst remaining in helpful mode. 'Works if you grip one between your knees,' he said. 'Or perhaps your partner can have one.'

'That won't work for him either.'

EXTRA WARNING: OMG (Old Medical Gag) alert

'Yes, it will. Works a treat. Put it in his shoe. It'll make him limp.'

The stern woman made another note; this time, almost breaking the lead of her pencil. The bell went for the end of visiting, and the incoming scrum reversed. The stern woman approached the nurses' station. Sternly.

'I'll be making a number of complaints, you know. Disgusting,' she growled, and stormed off as forthrightly as she had arrived.

'What was that about?' a puzzled Leanne asked.

'I think she used to be a nurse when Florence was a Nightingale. Shame she only wanted to pick holes in what we do. What a wealth of experience she must have had to share with the young nurses. Most of them are lovely, but there's always the odd one. By the way, did you weigh Mrs Higgins?'

'Oh yes, I was going to talk to you about that. She's lost a lot of weight this week – about 8 and a half kilos.'

Brian had an inkling of the cause of the sudden weight loss. 'Mmm. Have a look at the notes. What did she come in for?'

Leanne's face fell slowly, and she let out an embarassed giggle. 'Oh. Had a leg amputated. Whoops!'

'Don't think it'll catch on at Weight Watchers, do you?'

'Nah. 'elf 'n' safety. Might fall over.'

'Your risk assessment skills astound me.'

8. Admissions, General Bustle

4pm. A trolley trundled onto the ward, up from A&E and containing an elderly lady. Lucy introduced herself and, having gleaned brief details, summoned Chloe to help her transfer the new patient into a bed.

'This is Phyllis, just arrived from A&E. She's a breech.'

A fleeting thought caused Chloe to wonder whether maternity would not have been a better place for the patient. Unfortunately, the thought just managed to squeeze out past her teeth.

'A baby at her age? And an upside-down one as well? That's unusual.'

'No, not that sort of breech. She's just spent over four hours in A&E. Generally unwell. Came from respite care in residential accommodation.'

She turned to Phyllis and enquired how she came to be in her care.

On your feet with a hat of your choice: *Y.M.C.A.* - Village People

Old girl, have you come from a home? (tell me)
Old girl, with a room of your own (do you)
Old girl, do you care for yourself
Or just sit there de-hy-dra-ting?

Old girl, you've a big UTI (I said)
Old girl, you need 12-hour IVI
With potassium, then some trimethoprim
Or some ni-tro-fur-an-to-in.

Chloe popped a swab into Phyllis's nostril, and explained...

We're gonna check you for
M.R.S.A. (E-Coli, C-Diff and)
M.R.S.A.
Or is it ESBL, that's been giving you hell?
We'll check for it anyway.

Lucy continued...

Old girl, are you here for a laugh?
Could the care home not get any staff
For the weekend? It's a bank holiday
And they know you'll be looked after.

Later, when you're feeling more fit
Social workers can then do their bit
To assess you – do you need extra care
Or someone to do your shopping?

But first we'll check you for...
M.R.S.A. (E-Coli, C-Diff and)
M.R.S.A.
Or maybe ESBL has been giving you hell?
So we'll check for it anyway
M.R.S.A....

Site manager Debbie was passing and took up the case from her point of view...

> *Old girl, we've got targets to meet,*
> *So tomorrow you're back on your feet.*
> *If you're poorly, then come back next week*
> *And we'll try and re-admit you.*

> *Sorry, you must be on your way,*
> *We must cut down the average stay,*
> *Or the gov'ment will cut down our pay*
> *But we'll have a bed next Wednesday*

> *M.R.S.A...*

Sister Karen had had a busy day dealing with demands from above and issues on the ward. Sometimes she didn't know whether she was punched, bored, or countersunk. And the long 12-hour days were taking their toll. They were meant to alternate between clinical and management shifts, but they were usually congealed into one. She flopped down on a chair in her office.

Sing along to: *I Don't Like Mondays* - Boomtown Rats

> *The VitalPac* *inside my head*
> *Displays its battery low.*
> *But I'm on a 12-hour shift today,*
> *No way I'm gonna stay at home.*

> *And Debbie doesn't understand me,*
> *I've still got pills to do.*
> *I'm on a clinical day,*

---

* VitalPac: an iPhone-based device for monitoring patients' vital signs.

Not a management day,
And still got my writing to do.

(Wanna cry.)
I don't like long days.
(Wanna cry.)
I don't like long days.
(Wanna cry.)
I don't like long days.
Wish I was off-o-o-o-o-offffffff
To pastures new.

Where's Becky now, has Brian come back?
What time did they go to break?
Have they come back yet?
Can I go home yet?
Ev'ry man and his dog
Has phoned in sick.

And I'm not getting anywhere.
Any moment now I'll pull out my hair
Is it a management day
Or a clinical day?
And still the staff roster to do.

(Wanna cry.)
I don't like long days.
(Wanna cry.)
I don't like long days.
(Wanna cry.)
I don't like long days.
Wish I was off-o-o-o-o-offffffff
To pastures new, new, new, new.

I'm not on my mobile if anyone asks,
And it's not time to go home yet.
I can't be all things to all the people,
It's a 12-hour shift and I must not fret.
The consultants rattle,
The site manager cackles,
There's nothing more I can do.
Is it a clinical day
Or a management day?
I've not got a Scooby-Doo-oo-oo-oo-oo-ooh

(Wanna cry.)
I don't like long days.
(Wanna cry.)
I don't like long days.
(Wanna cry.)
I don't like, I don't like
(Wanna cry.)
I don't like long days.

(Wanna cry.)
I don't like, I don't like,
(Wanna cry.)
I don't like long days.
(Wanna cry.)
I don't like long days
Wish I was off-o-o-o-o-o-offffffff
To pastures new.

Composing and bracing herself in equal measure, Karen took a deep breath and ventured out once more onto the ward.

'Leanne, are you happy to do an ECG on Phyllis?'

'Nah. 'elf 'n' safety.'

Student Nurse Nicole, still in the first flush of enthusiasm, boldly stepped forward. 'No problem. I'll do it. I've done one before.'

She disappeared, wheeling the ECG trolley behind her like Bo-Peep and her sheep.

The ward was quieter. Staff walked about checking and chatting to patients. Lucy peered into a side room and gasped as she stared at an empty bed, which had been occupied the last time she'd looked. She searched about and asked colleagues if they'd noticed a mildly confused wanderer. Meanwhile, some of the crew were reflecting on the day so far. (Good luck with this one, if you're singing along. You may need help from a friend or choir.)

Get the big guns up for this next one: *Bohemian Rhapsody* – Queen

Is this our real life?
Or is it purgatory?
Caught in a treadmill
No escape from Emergency.
Open your eyes,
Roll them up to the skies and see.
I'm just a staff nurse,
I need some sympathy

Because in they come, out they go,
Some are high, some are low.

Anyway the sh*t flows
Always seems to land up... on me.

Lucy, in a professionally controlled state of panic,
approached Sister Karen...

Sister, I've lost a man
And I don't know where he's gone.
Didn't think he'd be this long.
Sister, he was so confused
Do you think I should have called security?
Sister, oo-oo-ooh.

Karen reassured her.

Don't you worry so
He'll be back in A&E this time tomorrow.
Carry on, carry on,
Do your observations.

Clinical site manager Debbie, though, had other ideas.

Too late, his bed has gone.
If he wants to come back, he
Will have to go through A&E.
Should've got the doctor, bleeped the SHO,
Got him written up for haloperidol.

Lucy was far from consoled.

Sister, oo-oo-ooh,
I don't wanna quit.
Sometimes wish I'd never been trained at all.

Was that the gentle strains of a guitar solo wafting through the ward as Care Assistant Chloe brought some slightly reassuring news?

I saw a glimpse of Mr. Scroggins through the window.
In a bush, in a bush, with his catheter akimbo.
Like a streak of lightning, very very frightening.
Wheee!

Everybody was wondering what to do next...

Debbie Morris (Debbie Morris) Debbie Morris
(Debbie Morris) Debbie Morris needs to know...
Bloody 'ell, no, no, no, no!

I'm just a staff nurse, nobody loves me.
(She's just a staff nurse from a small hospital
Spare her her PIN or she might have to go.)

Doctor Rock, Doctor Roe, who was it let him go?
This will not do, who was it let him go?
Doctor Roe! This will not... who was it let him go?
Doctor Roe! This will not...who was it let him go?
Doctor Roe! Who was it let him go? Doctor Roe!
Who was it let him go? Let him go-o-o-o-o.
Oh, Lucy Harris, Lucy Harris, Lucy Harris let him go!
I've messed it up! So will it be the sack for me,
for me, for meeeee...

The mystery guitarist struck up again, just as Mr Arthur Scroggins reappeared, catheter no longer akimbo, protesting...

So you think you can keep me locked up in here?
Away from my woman, my fags, and my beer?
Oh, no way. You're 'avin a laugh, pal, there's no way.
Just got to get out, just got to get right out of here.

With a last 'hurrah', in a desperate attempt to help them make it back to the plot, the guitarist played with a flourish until everything calmed down and Mr Scroggins was reinstated in his room, to the great relief of Staff Nurse Lucy, who sighed as she sang wistfully...

It's all such a hassle, anyone can see.
It's all such a hassle, and it always lands up on me.
Anyway the sh*t flows...

An important-looking lady with an even more important-looking lanyard appeared, holding an even MORE important-looking clipboard, and wearing inappropriate designer shoes. She passed the door of a side room.

'Nurse, can I have a bedpan?'
'Sorry, I'm from the CQC doing a continence audit. You need a nurse.' She sniffed, 'Could have said "please",' and set about her business with her important-looking clipboard.

Sister Karen also sniffed, but for a different reason.
'What's that burning smell?'
Nicole crept up to the nursing station looking sheepish.
'I think you'd better see Phyllis. I think she's on fire.'
They made their way to Phyllis's bay and slipped behind the curtain, from which was rising a small wisp of smoke.

'Show me what you did. Mmm... Ah. Next time, don't plug your patient into the mains. Perhaps an incident you could use for a reflective learning piece.'

'At least the lines were all straight, not waving all over the place. Looked so messy. She looks OK now, though, but the lines are wavy again.'

Sister Karen sighed. 'Your OCD is getting seriously disturbing. Now, are you happy admitting this patient just coming in? Remember: name, eye contact, and a smile. That says, "You are an individual, my attention is just on you, and it's going to be alright." You don't get a second chance to make a first impression.'

Two paramedics trundled their trolley onto the ward carrying another patient. Brian and Nicole were waiting. A paramedic spoke.

'This is Mrs Jones. Has had a cold for several weeks, but suddenly started spiking a temperature. Husband says she was very hot in bed last night.'

Brian and Nicole helped the patient into bed and started the admission paperwork. Nicole fetched Mrs. Jones a jug of water and Brian handed the woman the call button.

'Here's your room service button, Mrs Jones.'

'Room service, eh? Just like being in a hotel. I feel well looked after already.'

'I like all my guests to feel important. Just call if you need anything. We'll be along within a couple of hours. Sometimes it's even quicker than that.'

Not for the first time, Nicole looked a little puzzled.

'That's a bit weird. Guests? Two hours?'

'Just mad old me and a bit of cod psychology. If the patient is expecting us to answer in one minute and you take two, they're disappointed. If they're expecting five minutes and you respond in four, you exceed their expectations, and you've had more time to finish what you're doing and pay them full attention. So you look good, the ward looks good, and they speak well of the NHS when they tell their grandchildren about the time they were in hospital. And they will, because that's how significant a hospital stay is for most people. Remember that.

'We see hundreds of patients, but their own experience is usually a rare one, and individual to them. Trouble is, the press and politicians raise unrealistic expectations about the NHS, either to sell newspapers to people like Disgusted of Tunbridge Wells, or to get votes by pretending to sort it all out. As long as they can look good. Fortunately, most patients are more realistic.'

The afternoon settled into the general routine, slightly calmer than the morning, but busy enough with drinks rounds, general patient care, commodes, trips to scanning, visits by social workers, physiotherapists, and Occupational Therapists.

Site manager Debbie, however, was starting to feel the heat as she tried to find beds for everyone waiting in A&E or coming in by ambulance. She came in, flustered.

Have a crack to: *Eleanor Rigby* – The Beatles)

A&E's bursting, GP admissions are getting
more frequent each day,
Is there no other way?
See them all coming – heart attacks, strokes,
overdoses, and slightly unwell –
Feels just like hell.

All the poorly people, where do they all come from?
All the poorly people, where do they all belong?
I look at all the poorly people!
I look at all the poorly people!

There is no let-up, they keep coming in,
In the daytime and all through the night –
There is no respite.
Off their legs, chest pain, collapse query cause,
Cellulitis and gout –
Can't keep them out.

All the poorly people, where do they all come from?
All the poorly people, where do they all belong?
I look at all the poorly people!
I look at all the poorly people!

All the poorly people, where do they all come from?
All the poorly people, WHY CAN'T THEY ALL GO
HOME?!

Oblivious to all the activity, the important-looking
lady with the important-looking lanyard and the even
MORE important-looking clipboard, walked back

on her return journey in her important-looking, inappropriate designer shoes. She passed the side room again.

'Nurse.'

A plaintive voice drifted from the side room. For a moment, she thought it sounded vaguely familiar. She decided to answer it.

'Nurse.'
'Yes? Have you finished with the bedpan?'
'It's too late now,' whispered Janet.

The important...etc. lady ticked a box on her clipboard. 'That'll make their figures look bad,' she muttered, as she walked away.

9. Consultant Review

Dr Rock strolled in.

'Hello, Nurse, I've come to review the patient, Ted was his name. Had the chest X-ray. Oh, and Mr. Singh who had the DVT scan – looks positive.'

Becky accompanied him to the bay, where Ted was sitting up, looking a little better with his oxygen on. He had stopped coughing. Whether this was because Dr Rock had told him to stop, or whether the oxygen was doing its job, was uncertain. Dr Rock delivered his verdict and the plan of treatment.

Serving suggestion: *I Can See Clearly Now* – Johnny Nash

I can see through you now the rays have gone.
There are no obstacles in the way.
There are no tell-tale signs of shadowing,
You're gonna live (live) live for another day.

So this is the treatment that I would advise –
Put him on steroid meds for a week,
Four times a day he needs to nebulise,
And I will return (turn) turn and give it a tweak.

Dr Rock moved on briskly. He thought he may yet get his round of golf in before dinner.

'Now, where's Mr. Singh? Ah yes, bed 6. Good afternoon, Mr. Singh.'

'Good afternoon, Doctor. Did my scan show anything?'

(The next song may benefit from a backing vocalist singing the words in brackets.)

Try this tune: *1-2-3* – (Len Barry)

> *DVT – you've got a great big blood clot*
> *Above your knee.*
> *You need anticoagulation*
> *Therapy.*
> *(Tinzaparin, then some Warfarin)*
>
> *Holiday – you took a long-haul airline*
> *Direct to Bombay (OK, Mumbai, but it doesn't rhyme).*
> *Started to feel some leg pain while you were away.*
> *(Tried to ignore it, took no notice)*
>
> *Another flight. Came back to Gatwick airport*
> *Overnight,*
> *Pain was excruciating – gave you a fright.*
> *(Went to the doctor, had a D-dimer*)*

So it's a DVT, etc.

---

* D-Dimer: A blood test used when a deep vein thrombosis is suspected.

10. Quieter

Sometimes in the afternoon, after visiting and before the evening meal, there can be a perceptible reduction in the pace of activity. While the HCAs were checking patients on their comfort rounds, Becky heard some gentle sobbing. She went to ask Brenda what was upsetting her.

'Hello, Brenda. Is anything the matter?'

'No. It's alright. I'm just being silly.'

'Now, come on. You're upset about something. What's bothering you?'

'How am I going to manage? I've just been told I am diabetic. Will I lose my toes? I've heard such horrible stories about the complications you can have. My friend's dad lost a leg.'

'That's unlikely to happen to you if we can help you manage it. It's a bit of a shock suddenly having a diagnosis like that, but there is a lot we can do to reduce the chances of complications. We know about diabetes, and you know about yourself. So, if we can teach you enough about the condition, you'll become the expert on how it affects you, and how you can manage and control it. Have you got a few minutes?'

'Can't recall any pressing engagements in the next few minutes.' Brenda relaxed slightly. 'But you're much too busy.'

Becky looked her straight in the eye. 'Brenda, if I'm too busy for my patients, I'm too busy full stop. Let's have a little chat, and I'll get some information for you which may help. There's a lot to take in, so you won't do it all in one sitting, but I'll just go through some main points with you, and you can do the rest at your own pace. I'll do my best to answer any questions, then maybe ask one of my specialist colleagues to come and see you. I'm sure if we take some of the uncertainty away and make sure you know about the support available, you'll find it easier to move forward.'

'Thank you, Nurse.'

'It's Becky.'

'OK, Becky. Oh, you're so kind. Come here.'

Sometimes a hug said much more about patient care than words. Or audits.

Back in the fray, Brian was frustrated. Lucy was within range.

'That lady – Doris Wossname, the confused one – watch her. She's refusing all her food and tablets, threw her water all over me, swore, and tried to punch me. She grabbed one of the HCA's arms and dug her nails in while we were trying to put her into bed earlier.'

'Thanks for the warning. Has she got dementia?'

'Yes. But people can still be civil, can't they? The lady in the bed next door said she's been like a rattlesnake with piles since she came in.'

'Sounds a little harsh. Not sure I'd have put it like that. Let's see. She was rushed in from the care home at 5am after she fell out of bed, confused and agitated, with a suspected water infection. Has had blood tests, been taken for a CT scan, on a trolley for nearly 12 hours then shipped up to us. Not surprising she's a bit disoriented. The poor dear's probably absolutely terrified, wondering what on earth is happening. I'd be scared witless if it were me. I'll try and have a chat with her.'

'Best of luck.'

Lucy went to Doris. 'Hello, my name is Lucy. I'm one of the nurses. It's Doris, isn't it?'

'Why am I in this office?'

'This is a hospital, Doris. You came here because you're poorly.'

'No, I'm not. I want to go back to my dad's house.'

'You're in hospital, Doris. You fell over in the middle of the night. I think you must have been trying to get to the bathroom.'

This was all a bit too much for Doris. Tears of frustration welled up. 'I don't know where anything is. What's happening to me?'

Lucy offered a reassuring hand. 'Can you remember what happened to you?'

'I was a nurse.'

'Where did you work?'

'London. At the end of the war.'

'Bet things were different in your day, weren't they?'

'Yes. The doctors wore bow ties. Matrons were very strict. Didn't take any nonsense. But they helped you. They were good times. We made lots of lifelong friends, all being in the war and that.'

'There weren't as many tablets then, were there?'

'No.'

'Talking of tablets, I've got one or two for you. Would you like some help with them? Just some paracetamol to help with the aches and pains from your fall. There we are. And here's a drink to get them down. Now, it's nearly teatime. Shall we sit you up ready? There we are. Let's pop a pillow under that shoulder... Now, is that comfy? Here's your call button. Just press it if you need anything. We'll bring your tea along in a little while, and Chloe will help you with it. Will that be OK?'

'You seem to have so much paperwork now. In my day, we just had to look after people. But you're very kind.'

Lucy chuckled. 'You must have caught me on a good day.'

Brian walked past and caught Doris's eye.

'What a handsome young man.'

Lucy chuckled again. 'Wrong on two counts, I'm afraid Doris. If you keep saying that, we may have to sort you out a white stick.'

'Anyway, mustn't keep you. You'd better do your paperwork, or nobody will believe you've been here today.'

'You're right there, Doris. I'd better get on.' And Lucy sat down at the table.

'Nice one there, Lucy,' admired Brian. 'How did you do it?'

'I just hit on an area she remembered – a time in her life she was happiest – and went with the flow. We found some common ground, something we both understood.'

Lucy opened the first file and started her writing. *Why did it always seem a rush to get it done in time?*

And – relax to: (Sitting on the) *Dock of the Bay* – Otis Redding

> *Sitting at the desk in the bay,*
> *Filling in my charts every day,*
> *Watching all the patients come in,*
> *And I watch them go away again.*

> *I spend my time body mapping*
> *Into the VitalPac, tap-tap-tap-tapping,*
> *Putting observations in,*
> *Recording pulses blood pressures and pain.*

> *Sitting at the desk in the bay...*

> *I've got so much writing to do.*
> *Check the clock and it's four twenty-two.*
> *There's IVs and drips to put up,*
> *And filling all the water jugs up.*

> *Sitting at the desk in the bay...*

(Words: Claire Coote)

As was the custom, as soon she sat down to write, the call bells started. Lucy answered Brenda's bell.

'Could you fill my jug up again, please?'

'Yes, sure. But that's the third jug in 20 minutes. Are you diabetic?'

'Yes. Just diagnosed. Becky was explaining it all to me. It says in this booklet that diabetes can make you very thirsty.'

'You're certainly that! You're drinking like a fish!'

'I don't think so. I'm using a straw.'

'Silly old me. Whatever was I thinking? Fancy believing that fish drank through a straw!' They chuckled in unison.

An emergency call button crashed into the moment, and everyone else on the ward ran towards a side room. One by one, several call buttons went off.

Lucy, left on her own, rushed round with commodes, helping people back to bed, fetching water. Her feet were on fire for what seemed ages.

'Nurse, I need the toilet!'

'Nurse, can I have a drink?'

'Nurse, help me!'

'Nurse, that man's going to fall over!'

'Nurse, nur-r-se!'

'Nurse, Helllp!'

A man shoved his way past a patient unsteadily pushing a Zimmer frame.

'Let me through, I'm a diabetic!'

There was no let up. Lucy was grateful she could multi-task.

'Nurse, I need a drink.'

'Nurse, I want to get out!'

'Nurse, they're coming to kidnap me!'

'Nurse, I want a bedpan!'

'Nurse, can you peel me a grape?'

'Nurse, there are spiders all over me!'

'Nurse, can you just take away the pain and leave the swelling?'

Then, as abruptly as it had started, the emergency bell stopped. The staff returned to the ward. Lucy flopped onto a chair at the nurses' station.

11. End of the Day

Composing herself, Lucy sang her frustration.

Foxtrot time: *Please Release Me* – Engelbert Humperdinck

> *Please release me, send me home,*
> *Don't want to work here anymore.*
> *Don't want to see one more commode –*
> *Release me and send me down the road.*
>
> *Started out all bright and keen*
> *From nursing school, all squeaky clean.*
> *My brain was sharp and so alive.*
> *The most I do now is survive.*
>
> *I love the job – don't get me wrong,*
> *But maybe I've been here too long.*
> *So hear me now as I complain –*
> *Release me and let me live again.*

'That came from the heart,' observed Sister Karen.

'Oh, don't worry. I love the job; it's just that there are days when I don't like it. People seem to be getting ruder and more stroppy, there's so much more paperwork, and the goalposts seem to change every five minutes. If only the people who set the goalposts ever came onto a ward, met a real patient, and understood what they were managing – why we're all here. You know, people rather than just targets and money. Not just a state visit when the inspectors are due. Time a few of them got down here and found out what a patient looks like – walked the job once in a while. When push comes to shove, this job is simple: it's just one person looking after someone else. I know we have to have policies and procedures, but if anyone needs to worry about things like a dignity policy... if you need one of those, you've got the wrong people doing the job. The patients are fine – lovely most of the time. Although there's something disconcerting about a patient who knows too much about the world of aperients.'

'Not throwing in the towel then?'

'Oh, goodness no. I'll know when that time comes. If I can still do it with a smile on my face and keep learning, if I can still treat every patient as an individual and keep the sense of wonder about how we are made in the first place, I'll keep going until someone chucks me out.'

'So, you'll be back tomorrow?'

'Of course. I guess the floggings will continue until morale improves, but apart from anything else, I'd miss being part of this great team – us against the world. We generally pull together.'

'Sometimes even in the same direction.' Karen took her time over a wry smile. 'Home time?'

They exchanged looks, and both nodded.

'Yes. Got to do it all over again for the kids now.'

The day shift was ending. They sang together.

Go out with a bang: *We are the Champions* - Queen

We've given their pills, we've washed them all,
Even filled out a form for an incident after a fall.
It's been busy as ever, not much time for a rest,
And that woman in the corner bed has been such a pest.

But, we are the nurses, my friend,
And we'll keep on nursing till the end.
Tablets and potions; commodes, drips, and lotions.
Not for the nervous, 'cos we are the nurses on the ward.

We've completed our shift, we've passed the test,
Done resuscitation on someone who had an arrest.
It's been no easy stroll, no walk in the park.
Now our colleagues have to do it again,
This time in the dark,

For we are the nurses...

-oOo-

12. Epilogue

In conclusion, I have included some material for thought. This is not a textbook, so there is minimal comment or judgement on the content. Care of the older patient and those with impaired cognition is a fundamental part of nursing, and quality care surely comes from the character and attitude of the practitioner, rather than through a policy. Over to you...

First, a confession. The diagram on the next page started life as a doodle in a particularly tedious lecture during my nursing training. Despite its inauspicious origin, I have added to it over the years, and as this has happened it seems to have grown in sense and relevance in life and wider society. In nursing, reflection may offer insight and understanding of the older patient, possibly with dementia. In a wider context, the human lifecycle has fundamental implications for fiscal planning, health, and social care.

The normal distribution curve is the base for the diagram, although its shape is variable – influenced by factors such as the duration of education and health advances which enable people to live longer, although with multiple comorbidities.

This knowledge has probably been out there for a long time, but perhaps not in this graphic form.

The Human Life Cycle

Human Life Cycle Diagram

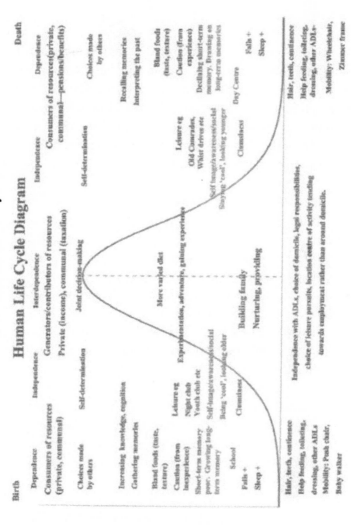

Birth					Death
Dependence	Independence	Interdependence	Independence		Dependence
Consumers of resources (private, communal)	Self-determination	Generators/contributors of resources Private (income), communal (taxation)	Self-determination		Consumers of resources (private, communal)—pensions/benefits)
Choices made by others		Joint decision-making			Choices made by others
	Increasing knowledge, cognition Gathering memories				Recalling memories Interpreting the past
Bland foods (taste, texture)		More varied diet			Bland foods (taste, texture)
Caution (from inexperience)		Experimentation, adventure, gaining experience		Leisure eg Old Comrades, WIslr drives etc	Caution (from experience)
Short-term memory poor. Growing long-term memory	Leisure eg Night club Youth club etc				Declining short-term memory. Drawing on long-term memories
	Self-image/awareness/social Being 'cool', looking older	Building family Nurturing, providing		Self-image/awareness/social Staying 'cool', looking younger	
School	Cleanliness		Cleanliness	Day Centre	
Falls +					Falls +
Sleep +					Sleep +

Hair, teeth, continence
Help feeding, toileting, dressing, either ADLs
Mobility: Pram chair, Baby walker

Independence with ADLs, choice of domicile, legal responsibilities, choice of leisure pursuits, location centre of activity tending towards employment rather than around domicile.

Hair, teeth, continence
Help feeding, toileting, dressing, either ADLs.
Mobility: Wheelchair, Zimmer frame

Dementia

The following article reports early research from 1999. I have included it as it appeared. without further comment. There are just two questions which may start your reflection: What is the difference between 'child-*ish*' and 'child-*like*'? Is there anything to apply from this?

BBC News, Wednesday, August 19th, 1999
Published at 10.59 BST

Health: Alzheimer's 'a second childhood'

People with Alzheimer's disease would be happier if they were treated as infants instead of adults, researchers have said.

They said dementia could indeed be a form of second childhood, after they found that people with the disease lost essential skills in the same order in which they developed them as a child.

As Alzheimer's progresses, sufferers find it increasingly difficult and then impossible to perform even the simplest everyday tasks – such as washing, eating, and dressing – without supervision.

However, a leading charity has said it may be dangerous to treat people who have lived a full life as children.

'Patients can be happy'

The findings of the study, which was conducted over 20 years, was presented at an international conference of specialists in the disease in Vancouver.

Dr Barry Reisberg, the outgoing president of the International Psychogeriatric Association, led the study.

He said: "Alzheimer's patients actually can be happy and right now there are hundreds of thousands, perhaps millions, who are suffering because we do not know how to care for them."

The World Health Organisation estimates that 15 million people worldwide have the disease. *(Note: this was in 1999)*

Reverse order

Dr Reisberg said researchers at New York University found that Alzheimer's patients lost physical and mental abilities in exactly the opposite order that children gain them.

Eventually, they return to an infant-like state, he said, and compared adults in the advanced stages of Alzheimer's to children under two years old – able to smile but unable to speak or walk.

The researchers labelled the process 'retrogenesis'.

Dr Reisberg said the public sees a correlation between the problems of old age and those of children.

Literary precedent

The researchers noted that Shakespeare talked of 'second childishness' in *As You Like It*, and Aristophanes wrote that 'old men are children twice over'.

They suggest that if Alzheimer's patients were treated like infants, they would endure less physical suffering, but so far only 'adult measures' have been applied.

"It's not a matter of increasing resources. It's a matter of knowing what to do," Dr Reisberg said.

Potentially dangerous approach

The Alzheimer's Disease Society said the research was interesting but was unhappy with elderly patients being treated as children.

"We don't think it's OK to treat people who've lived a very long life, who have a wealth of experience and who've done a lot with their lives, as children," a spokeswoman said.

"That might be quite a dangerous thing to do."

Full original paper: Reisberg, B. et al. Towards a Science of Alzheimer's Disease Management: A Model Based Upon Current Knowledge of Retrogenesis, International Psychogeriatrics Vol 11 No.1 1999 pp7-23

'Each one had their own stories to tell'

Alf

Alf was born in 1920, shortly after his father returned from the First World War – one of the lucky ones. He had a happy childhood, with loving parents who managed to balance firm discipline with a lot of love and attention; even in the hard times of the Great Depression, the family was adequately provided for – no luxuries, but boosted by the attitudes and care that money cannot buy.

After the Second World War broke out, Alf was called up and later posted to Singapore. In 1942, after the surrender to the Japanese, he found himself working on the infamous Burma 'death' Railway. The values passed on from his father sustained his sanity and self-respect through unimaginable hardship, deprivation, and even torture. At the end of hostilities, he returned to England, married, and started a family. Alf led a settled, stable life working as an electrician. He tried to pass on to his children the things he valued and that he had inherited from his father – humility, reliability, respect for others, hard work. He didn't 'do' PC, as it is known now. He just took everyone as he found them, recognising but not judging the good and bad in everybody from whatever background or station in life they came. The thoughts and dreams that often tormented him from his war did not define him; he kept them to himself for the sake of those he loved.

Outside work and family, he became involved in youth activities. In 30 years as a scout leader, he saw many boys – and later girls – grow into young adults of character, always quietly supporting and inspiring them to become the best they could be as they started to make their way in the world. The same applied to his kids and grandkids.

He never forgot that proudest of days at Buckingham Palace when he received his MBE from the Queen, but never made a big thing of it. He was just playing his part in helping the next generation, and someone had noticed.

As he moved into old age, his health started to decline, and he found himself reluctantly needing care from those he had cared for. He resolutely did as much as he could, but was quick to graciously acknowledge the help he received from his loved ones and those who looked after him in hospital, where his care was exemplary – a fact he was not shy of praising. He died what would be described as a 'good' death – comfortable, peaceful, all his boxes ticked, and with those he loved at his bedside.

He would have turned 100 this year. The best dad and 'Gramps' ever. His granddaughter adored him and felt his presence and strength daily, even now.

'You helped me be the best I can be. Love you. Miss you, Gramps,' whispered Becky.

Acknowledgements

Thanks to all the suppliers of raw material – intentional or otherwise, including Pam C 'just stop coughing'; Kim L 'wouldn't know the colour of the buckets'; Sian J 'if I was I wouldn't be'; Carol VDW 'let me through, I'm a diabetic'; unnamed Healthcare Assistant 'blue is SO not your colour'; and many others. Thanks to Tracey R for moving jobs and inspiring 'I Don't Like Long Days'.

Thanks to those who have read and critiqued the drafts – Vicci M, Carol VDW, Sally and Dawn, Deborah, Helen, Judith, Carole-Dawn, and others who have had a peep.

Thanks to Peter Clayton for his brilliant cover drawing.

Thanks to my dad, Roy Pencavel (first name Leonard), for my *nom-de-plume*. He would be 100 as well...

Thanks to Ilan Butler (Rogue Marketing) for the website.

Thanks to Dean, Tanis, Julie, and the team at Grosvenor House Publishing for their help, advice, and proofreading - for doing the heavy lifting in getting this book onto the page.

And thanks for buying this book (both of you).

If I've missed anyone, I crawl on my belly and beat myself with twigs, but you're appreciated nonetheless.

I'll stop now; this isn't the Oscars. I'll save that for the movie. If I write any more, I'll run out of space on the pa

Other books
by this author

There aren't any.

However, he did do a pantomime a few years ago.

And

'Who's the Diabetic Fish?' has also been written in the (original) form as a musical and as scripts for live, video screenplay, and audio formats. (If you would like to collaborate, please pop a message on the website.)

**To find out more, or keep in touch, go to
www.diabeticfish.com**

Who's the
Diabetic Fish?

Reviews you may not have seen

'Makes *Fifty Shades of Grey* look like a Nobel prize contender.' – E.L. Jones

A Wonderbra of a book! Really uplifting. - Anon

'This book stands as a fine example of the problems of folk with too much time on their hands.' MINDer

'That read was an hour of my life I'll never get back.' Ray Leonardsson

'It made me come over quite peculiar. I turned in my grave – and then smiled.' Nightingale, F. (Ms)

'Couldn't put it down – tried to flush three times and it still wouldn't go.' Local Recycling Service

'If you've read Adam Kay's *This is Going to Hurt*, don't bother with this. It's s**te.' Alan Koi

'This is a fake book. If I had written it, it would have been the greatest book in the history of literature.' Donald Trumpet

'Who stole my whiskers? Is it Tuesday?' Lt-Col Horace Worthington-Smythe, Bt (Ret'd)

'Wish I'd watched the paint drying instead.' C-D N

Lightning Source UK Ltd.
Milton Keynes UK
UKHW011833201021
392530UK00001B/20

9 781839 757099